To Capture the Wind

Sheila MacGill-Callahan

paintings by *Gregory Manchess*

Dial Books for Young Readers *New York*

Published by Dial Books for Young Readers
A Division of Penguin Books USA Inc.
375 Hudson Street
New York, New York 10014
Text copyright © 1997 by Sheila MacGill-Callahan
Pictures copyright © 1997 by Gregory Manchess
Designed by Nancy R. Leo
Printed in the U.S.A. on acid-free paper
First Edition
1 3 5 7 9 10 8 6 4 2

Library of Congress Cataloging in Publication Data
MacGill-Callahan, Sheila.
To capture the wind / Sheila MacGill-Callahan; paintings by Gregory Manchess.
p. cm.
Summary: In a risky plan to free her kidnapped lover, Oonagh cleverly solves
the evil pirate king's riddles, unites the princess Ethne with her lover, and invents sails.
ISBN 0-8037-1541-2 (trade).—ISBN 0-8037-1542-0 (library)
[1. Riddles—Fiction. 2. Pirates—Fiction. 3. Sailing—Fiction. 4. Inventions—Fiction.]
I. Manchess, Gregory, ill. II. Title.
PZ7.M16765Ho 1997   [E]—dc20   93-45966   CIP   AC r94

The art for this book was prepared using oil paints on canvas.

◆◆◆◆◆

The four riddles are taken from "Candlelight Carol" by John Rutter.
Copyright © 1985 by Oxford University Press.
Subpublished in North America by Hinshaw Music, Inc. Used by permission.

This one is for Evelyn, Rodney, Bruce, and Maria
—S.M-C.

To my daughter, Kelly, and my granddaughter, Breana
—G.M.

Oonagh was happy. Her sheep gave the best wool. Her fields grew the best corn. Her apples were unmatched in all Ulster. And on May Day she was to marry Conal, whose fame as a weaver spread far and wide across the land.

But one fine March evening when Oonagh came home from market, neighbors told her that the warriors of Malcolm, the pirate king of the islands, had come and dragged Conal from his loom and ridden away with him.

Oonagh set out at once to find Conal. The trail was not hard to follow. In every village the pirates had kidnapped only those noted for their skill in sewing and weaving.

When Oonagh came to the shore, she saw a maiden sitting by the edge of the water. Her eyes were red with weeping.

"Greetings, stranger," said Oonagh. "Have you seen the warriors of Malcolm, the pirate king?"

"Aye," said the maiden. "They embarked for Malcolm's isle this morning with their captives."

"And you did nothing?"

"What could I do? One person against five-and-twenty armed men."

There was truth in her answer. "By what name may I call you?"

"Ethne, daughter of Queen Brigid of the South."

"What is a southern princess doing on our shores?"

"Malcolm's son, Aidan, and I love each other, but I failed the test of four riddles that Malcolm gives any woman who seeks his son's hand in marriage."

"I'm good at riddles," Oonagh said. "Tell me what Malcolm will ask."

Ethne said, "The penalty for failure is seven years of slavery. I have served my seven years and was left here on the shore."

Oonagh placed a comforting arm around her. "Tell me all you know."

"There are four riddles. Three of them do not matter, but you *must* answer the first one correctly. I dare not tell you what it is, or Malcolm will place a curse on Aidan and he will die."

Oonagh was troubled. Did she love Conal enough to risk seven years of slavery? By moonrise she had made her decision.

She loaded a boat with wool and flax. By dawn she reached Malcolm's isle.

In the great hall Malcolm crouched like a toad on a throne of ivory. Aidan sat beside him and Conal stood behind Aidan's chair.

"State your business, Oonagh, daughter of Maire."

Oonagh did not look at Conal. "I seek the hand of Prince Aidan."

"You know the conditions?"

"I do."

"Very well. Here are four riddles. Answer one a week in any order or form you choose. Listen well:

How do you capture the wind on the water?
How do you count all the stars in the sky?
How can you measure the love of a mother?
How can you write down a baby's first cry?

"For the next twenty-eight days you will be my guest," Malcolm said.

"Agreed," Oonagh answered. "I brought Ulster wool and flax to be woven for my marriage. May I speak with your master weaver?"

"He stands behind Aidan's chair." Malcolm scowled at Aidan. "On your feet, boy. Greet your lady."

"She's not my lady and never will be!"

The king's face purpled with rage. "Stop mooning over that southern lass. For the next four weeks I order you to treat Oonagh with respect. When she fails, you may do with her what you will."

"You had better mend your manners before you marry me," Oonagh declared. She beckoned to Conal, "Attend me, fellow."

"Go with them," the king ordered Aidan.

Conal led Oonagh to a boxwood maze in the center of the garden. There Aidan found her in Conal's embrace.

She smiled at the startled prince. "Conal is my love, but Ethne awaits you on the shore. We have four weeks to outwit the king. Why does he need weavers and needle workers?"

Aidan laughed bitterly. "Greed and pride. He is the richest island lord, now his castle must be the most beautiful."

During the first week the spindles and looms sang from sunrise until dark.

On the seventh day Oonagh stood before the king.

"Which riddle have you chosen?" he asked.

"'How can you measure the love of a mother?' The answer is easy. A mother's love cannot be measured, for it has no bounds."

Malcolm roared his approval. "Answer the other three as ably and I'll be proud to call you my daughter."

Another week went by. If the pirates had paused in their feasting, they would have seen the slaves creep out by night to the harbor.

On the day of the second question Malcolm called Oonagh to him. "What is your choice?" Malcolm asked.

"'How do you count all the stars in the sky?' You don't. The only star that counts is the one in the north that guides the sailors home."

The king smiled at Oonagh. "Tonight you shall be my guest at the high table."

During the third week the needle workers never raised their heads from their tasks.

Once more Oonagh stood before the throne.

"Let me guess," said Malcolm. "Today you will tell me why you cannot capture the wind on the water."

"No. Today I will tell you that a baby's first cry cannot be written down, for it is the cry of life itself."

Malcolm threw a golden chain around her neck and called her "Daughter."

The fourth week the wind blew from the east. At night the slaves crept to the shore with bundles in their hands.

On the last day Oonagh fastened Aidan's sword beneath her cloak.

"Come with me to the harbor," she told the king. "The whole kingdom is gathered to hear my answer."

The pirates lounged on the dock. The slaves waited in small boats on the choppy water.

"Tell me how to capture the wind on the water and I'll be proud to wed you to my son," said Malcolm.

Oonagh backed to the edge of the pier where Conal and Aidan's boat waited below. "You said I could answer in any way I choose. I choose to show you."

She drew the sword ready to jump into the boat and cut the lines, when suddenly the wind dropped!

Malcolm shrank from the naked steel in her hand. "Seize her," he roared. "She has dared to draw upon me!"

A hundred blades flashed in the sunlight as Oonagh leaped into the boat.

"Row," she cried as she slashed the line, "row for our lives!"

The slaves grasped the oars they had made at night, and bent their backs to the stroke. The swordsmen gave way to the archers and a flight of arrows sped across the water.

"After them," yelled the king, but to no avail. The boats left on the shore had holes driven in their bottoms. The hail of arrows increased when the pirates discovered there was no way to pursue the fugitives.

"I love you, Oonagh," said Conal, "and if I die here, I die content." Blood was running down his arm where it had been pierced by an arrow, but still he rowed strongly.

Suddenly there was a puff of wind from the east, and then another. Oonagh stood to give a signal. Malcolm's jaw fell open in amazement as white, blue, and scarlet wings blossomed over the boats.

Oonagh made a trumpet of her hands. "'How do you capture the wind on the water?' Here is your answer, Malcolm. They have no name, but I call them 'sails.' A new word for a new idea."

The wind stood fair for Ulster. Oonagh and Conal, Aidan and Ethne were feasted in every village. On May Day they came to Oonagh and Conal's home place where all were gathered for the wedding.

It was a double wedding. The party afterward went on for nine days, and each day was better than the one before.

As for Malcolm, everyone laughed at him and refused to follow him. He gave up pirating and became an honest merchant. When Aidan and Ethne's first child was born, they made their peace with him and he became the proudest grandfather in all of Ireland.

MacGill-Callahan, Sheila
To Capture the Wind

DATE	ISSUED TO

MacGill-Callahan, Sheila
To Capture the Wind